THE MARSHMALLOW MAN

Illustrations copyright © 2009 by Stephen Macquignon
and 4RV Publishing

Book design by Aidana WillowRaven

ISBN-13: 978-0-9825886-2-8

Printed in the United States of America.

THE MARSHMALLOW MAN

written by Rena Jones

illustrated by Stephen Macquignon

Edmond, Oklahoma

Dedicated to my boys, Nathan & Neil, who brought
The Marshmallow Man to life

Once upon a time, there was a little old lady who lived by herself in a small house in the forest. She was lonely and wanted a friend.

"I don't have a friend, so I'll make one." she said. She formed his body out of fluffy white marshmallows. She used chocolate chips for his eyes and nose. For his mouth, she curled up a piece of red licorice. Finally, she gave him a bow tie made from a fruit roll and buttons made out of jelly beans. The little old lady admired her new friend. He looked yummy. Magically, the little marshmallow man came to life.

He looked up at the little old lady. "Please don't eat me," he cried. The marshmallow man jumped up and hopped out the window.

The little old lady ran after the marshmallow man. "Come back. Come back," she pleaded, but the marshmallow man did not come back.

He ran on saying, "Run, run, run, as fast as you can. You can't catch me, I'm the marshmallow man."

The marshmallow man ran through the forest where he spotted a rabbit sipping a cup of hot cocoa.

"Stop. Stop," shouted the rabbit. "I want to put you in my cocoa."

4

The marshmallow man did not stop.
He just laughed and ran on saying,
"Run, run, run, as fast as you can.
You can't catch me,
I'm the marshmallow man."

5

A little further he met a deer eating a bowl of crispy cereal.

"Wait. Wait!" hollered the deer. "I want to make crispy treats out of you."

6

The marshmallow man did not wait. He ran on saying, "Run, run, run, as fast as you can. You can't catch me, I'm the marshmallow man."

The deer began to chase the marshmallow man, followed by the rabbit, who was followed by the little old lady.

The marshmallow man was too fast for them and kept on running.

The marshmallow man came to a bear. The bear was sitting by a campfire poking it with a stick.

"Come here. Come here," demanded the bear. "I want to roast you on my fire."

8

The marshmallow man did not come there. He ran on saying ,
"Run, run, run,
as fast as you can. You can't catch
me, I'm the marshmallow man."

The bear joined the chase,
followed by the deer,
which was followed by the rabbit,
who were all followed by the little old lady.

The marshmallow man just
laughed and kept on running.

The marshmallow man came to a river. "Oh no," he cried. "They will catch me for sure. How can I get across the river?"

A sly fox appeared from behind a tree. "I can help you cross the river," said the fox.

"You won't eat me?" the marshmallow man asked.

"Of course not," the fox said. "I will help you, so jump on my tail."

11

The marshmallow man jumped on the fox's tail, and they began to cross the river.

"You are heavy, and I am getting tired," the fox grumbled as he waded through the water. "Jump on my back, and we can keep going," he said. The marshmallow man did as he was told. The water got deeper, and the marshmallow man was frightened.

"Jump on my nose, and you will stay dry," said the fox. So again, the marshmallow man did as he was told and jumped on the fox's nose.

The fox reached the other side of the river and walked on shore. Without a warning, the fox tossed the marshmallow man high in the air. Just as the marshmallow man was about to land in the hungry fox's mouth, he was caught by a hand.

"Bad fox," the little old lady scolded.

"It is a good thing I found a bridge," she said. "You would have been eaten by that sly fox, my friend."

The little old lady took the marshmallow man home.

"I will make you a warm bed," she said. "You must be tired from all that running."

She put a graham cracker down and placed the marsh-mallow man on top. "You need a blanket," she said. Getting a square of chocolate from her cupboard, she put it over the marshmallow man.

"There you go," she said. The marshmallow man fell fast asleep.

The little old lady looked at her friend. She was so hungry, and he looked so yummy. Quickly, she gobbled up the little marshmallow man -- bed and all!

"Oh, dear," she said. "My friend is gone, so I will make S'MORE friends."

Rena Jones

Rena Jones has always loved writing. Her favorite subjects in school were English and typing. As a teenager, she was involved in pen palling and wrote to more than 100 people from all over the world. She created several pen pal related newsletters in the early 1990s – one for pet lovers, another for coffee drinkers and a Christian-based one. By doing the newsletters, she was able to connect people to others who enjoyed writing letters as much as she did.

Rena is a home educator and has been teaching her children for 11 years. Her interests include photography, kayaking, camping, visiting national parks, wildlife watching and music. She lives in Bigfork, Montana with her husband, four children and two cats. When she's not writing, she's usually being entertained by the crazy wildlife that frequents her mountain home.

A New Job for Dilly was her first published work. *The Marshmallow Man* is her second with 4RV publishing.

http://home.centurytel.net/RickRena/index.html

Stephen Macquignon

Stephen Macquignon primarily works in the medium of pen and ink and color digitally. Stephen has been privileged to work with Director Michael Sporn of Michael Sporn Animation Inc. Also he is a monthly contributor for Stories for Children Magazine.

www.jacketflap.com/StephenM
http://scketch2color.multiply.com

CPSIA information can be obtained
at www.ICGtesting.com
Printed in the USA
LVHW071513010319
609192LV00011BA/206/P

9 780982 588628